Hilda Kalap is a Devon-based author and 'Donna and Dermot on the Move' is her first published picture book. She has been writing since she was a child inspired by the hedgerows, forests and the natural world on her doorstep.

Hilda is a single parent with two children, which keeps her very busy. In her free time she enjoys walking, yoga and meditation, having a massage, and playing the piano, albeit badly.

Donna and Dermot
on the Move

Hilda Kalap

Donna and Dermot on the Move

Nightingale Books

A CIP catalogue record for this title is
available from the British Library.

ISBN 978 1 90755 299 1

Nightingale Books is an imprint of
Pegasus Elliot MacKenzie Publishers Ltd.
www.pegasuspublishers.com

First Published in 2017

Nightingale Books
Sheraton House Castle Park
Cambridge England

Printed & Bound in Great Britain

Dedication

This book is dedicated to the real Donna and Dermot.

Acknowledgements

Hilda would like to acknowledge: My inspiring children, Elsa and Sylvie, who keep me smiling; and my friend Helen Alvarez, who saw this book at its earliest stage and gave me invaluable advice on how to make it better.

Jamie would like to acknowledge: My mum and dad, who always encourage me to follow my heart and my dreams.

Donna always had a smile
on her face.

Even when...

She fell off her bike and
grazed her knee...

She tripped on her rollerskates
and her tooth fell out...

Her big brother,
George, pulled her hair...

It rained and no rainbows
appeared, just huge
grey clouds...

Her grandparents visited
and ate the last piece
of cake...

Her smile was always there.
It had been there from the moment
she was born.

Donna was most smiley
when she was with her dog, Dermot.
They had such fun together.

They would run through
cornfields and hide in the
long grass.

They would watch the
swallows skimming the lake.

They would camp in a tent at the
end of the garden.

Then, one day, Donna's parents
got new jobs in the city.
They moved house, far away.

The air was smoky.
There were lots of cars and shops.
And people.
For the first time, Donna's
smile was gone.

Donna missed her friends.
She missed her grandparents.
She missed the cornfields
and the swallows.

She missed the clean air
and the big trees.
She lay on her bed feeling glum.

Donna made a plan; she'd
save her pocket money and take
the train back to her grandparents'
house in the country.

One day, it rained. There was a beautiful rainbow right over Donna's house. Dermot nudged her.

But Donna was too busy
counting the pocket money
in her jam jar to pay attention.

One night, the stars shone
so brightly they lit Donna's house
a glittery gold. Dermot pointed
at them with his paw.

But Donna was too busy
thinking about the swallows
and the lake to notice.

One day, the neighbours' children
asked if she wanted to play.
They had a slide and a treehouse
in their garden.

But Donna was busy crossing off
the days on the calendar,
counting down to when she would
be back at her grandparents' house.

And that day finally arrived...
the jam jar was full!

Donna opened the front door
with her little bag all packed
and Dermot next to her
on his lead. And then...

She heard the most amazing
sound you could imagine.
Joyful music with drums,
a guitar, and singing. Like angels.

And where was it coming from?
A carnival procession on their street.
There were the neighbours,
and George, and right at the
front were her grandparents
and her mum and dad.

She remembered her parents sewing and
painting one night.
She had been too busy to pay
much attention.

They were all right here, now.
Suddenly Dermot licked her face and Donna
stopped thinking about the past.
She was with them too, here and now.
It was the brightest, happiest moment.

Now was better than any other time.
Donna stepped out into the street.
She didn't want to miss a thing.
She smiled.

The smile grew bigger.
It felt like the smile had never gone away...
had always been there... all the while.